The Way
of the Willow Branch

EMERY BERNHARD

Illustrated by
DURGA BERNHARD

Gulliver Books
Harcourt Brace & Company
San Diego   New York   London

Requests for permission to make copies of any part of the work
should be mailed to: Permissions Department,
Harcourt Brace & Company, 6277 Sea Harbor Drive,
Orlando, Florida 32887-6777.

Gulliver Books is a registered trademark of Harcourt Brace & Company.

Library of Congress Cataloging-in-Publication Data
Bernhard, Emery.
The way of the willow branch / Emery Bernhard;
illustrated by Durga Bernhard.
p.   cm.
Summary: An old branch falls from a willow tree and has many
adventures before eventually becoming part of a young boy's mobile.
ISBN 0-15-200844-6
[1. Trees—Fiction.] I. Bernhard, Durga, ill. II. Title.
PZ7.B45518Way   1996
[E]—dc20   95-9977

First edition
A B C D E

Printed in Singapore

The paintings in this book were done in Winsor & Newton gouache
and colored pencil on Whatman 140-lb. cold-press watercolor paper.
The display type was set in Blackfriar.
The text type was set in Weiss.
This book was printed with soya-based inks on Leykam recycled paper,
which contains more than 20 percent postconsumer waste and has a
total recycled content of at least 50 percent.
Color separations by Bright Arts, Ltd., Singapore
Printed and bound by Tien Wah Press, Singapore
Production supervision by Warren Wallerstein and Ginger Boyer
Designed by Durga Bernhard and Lydia D'moch

To our friends and neighbors in the Hollow,
Marguerite and Nadir, who follow the Way . . .

and to their dogs,
Surya, Punga, and Gita,
who love to pick up sticks

All night a storm blows and shakes the branches of a great willow tree. The tree dances and sways in the wind.

Just before dawn, an old branch breaks off
and falls to the earth.

A dog nosing along the ground snatches up the willow branch.

The dog trots over to a boy and drops it at
his feet. "Fetch!" shouts the boy.

The branch flips through the air and splashes into the stream.

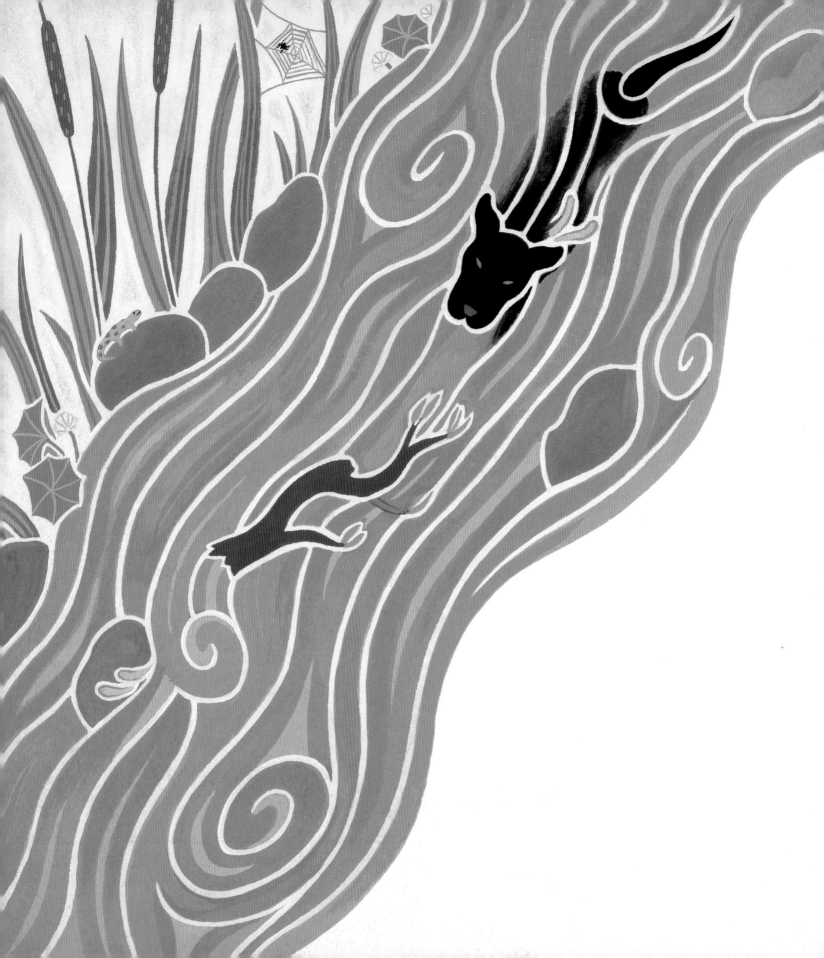

The dog plunges into the water and paddles after the branch, but the stream is swollen and its current is swift. The willow branch floats just out of reach, drifts under the bridge, and slips away.

Caught in eddies and swirls, then spinning free, the willow branch skims over stones and glides through reeds until it tangles in the limbs of an old fallen oak.

A beaver pops up her head and seizes the branch. She drags it onto a thick mound of mud and sticks, but the stream is still rising. The water surges, lifting the willow branch and carrying it away.

Now the stream runs slow and clear. Caught
between boulders, its soggy bark peeling,
the willow branch steams in the sun.

An osprey swoops low and grabs the branch.
She flaps away to a bulky nest of sticks and
leaves high above the stream.

The mother osprey perches on the willow branch while she feeds her young. When the young birds are ready to fly, they grip the branch, spread their wings, and glide away.

Before winter's first storm, the ospreys are gone. A fierce, chill wind rushes through the valley and claws at the cliff.

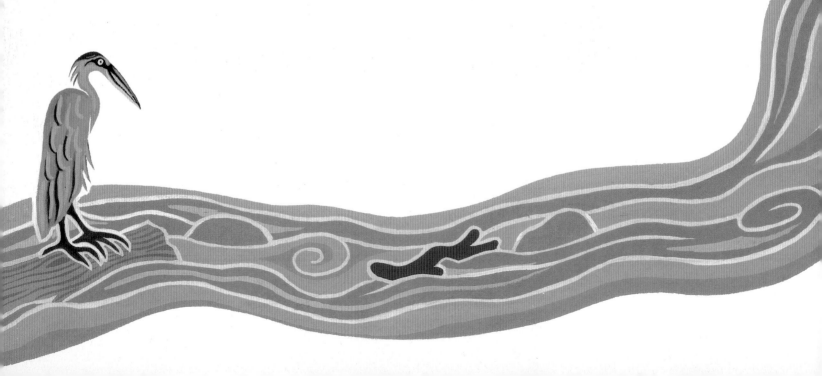

The nest falls, breaking apart in the cold, dark water. Each stick goes its own way. The willow branch glides swiftly downstream and into a deep river.

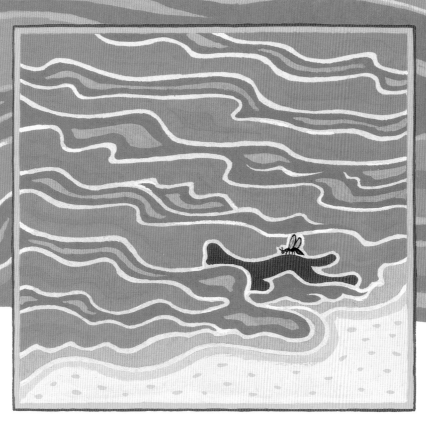

A speedboat knifes through the water. Its rippling wake wafts the branch onto a sandy bank.

A girl stops to pick up the willow branch. Singing to herself, she draws in the sand, then throws the branch back in the river.

The river flows into the sea, and for a long time the willow branch drifts, tossed and pitched, warped and worn, smoothed and shaped by the ocean waves.

Far from land, the branch is caught in a net and hauled aboard
a boat. A fisherman untangles the branch from the wet rope.
He casts it back into the sea and watches it disappear.

One day, the willow branch is lifted in the
crest of a big wave and washed up on a dry,
sunny beach.

A dog bounds over to the willow branch and brings it to a beachcombing boy.

The boy wrestles with the dog and tugs the branch from his jaws. It is now bare driftwood. "Perfect," says the boy, turning the branch around and around. He smiles and puts it into his bucket.

Shells and starfish, driftwood and feathers, pinecones and pebbles are all spread on the kitchen table to dry. The boy drills holes and ties knots, then loops string around the willow branch. He moves the objects here and there until everything dangles just right.

The boy's mother hangs the new mobile over
his bed. "I wonder where this driftwood came
from?" she asks, watching the willow branch
wobble and turn.

All night the wind blows, whistling through
trees and rattling windows. Inside, over faintly
clinking seashells, the willow branch floats
on the soft nighttime air, always home . . .
and always on its way.

How to Make Your Own Mobile

To make this mobile you'll need a pair of scissors and string, yarn, or strong thread, preferably in different colors. You'll also need a grown-up helper.

Collect a few pebbles, shells, pinecones, feathers, or other interesting small objects.

Find three firm sticks or small pieces of driftwood (they should be at least as thick as a pencil). One of the sticks should be about a foot long, and the other two should be about six inches long.

Cut a piece of string that is twice as long as your longest stick. Tie the two ends of the string to the two ends of the longest stick.

Hold your stick by the string and hang it up on a doorknob while you work on the rest of the mobile.

Choose five of your favorite objects. Cut five different lengths of string no shorter than six inches. Tie the strings around the objects, or ask your grown-up helper to drill small holes in objects that can be pierced, and tie the strings through the holes. (A hand drill with a small bit works best.)

Tie the heaviest object to the middle of the long stick hanging from the doorknob. Tie each of the other four objects to the four ends of the two shorter sticks.

Cut two more pieces of string, each about a foot long. Tie one end of each string to the ends of the long stick. Loosely tie the other end of each string to the middle of the two short sticks (you should be able to slide the loops back and forth).

Balance your mobile by sliding the strings back and forth along the two short sticks until everything "dangles just right." Make sure all three sticks are roughly level.

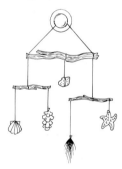

Cut one long string to hang your mobile (ask your grown-up helper to measure with you). Loop this long string through the string that holds your mobile. With your grown-up helper, find a safe place to hang your mobile. Good places are near a window, over a bed, on a porch, or in a place where the mobile will cast shadows on the wall.

Watch your mobile. Even a slight air current will be enough to make a balanced mobile move.